W9-BIA-777

ROCKFORD PUBLIC LIBRARY
3 1112 01520452 8

Bah! Humbug?

Lorna & Lecia Balian

Star Bright Books
New York

Published in the United States of America by Star Bright Books, Inc., New York.
The name Star Bright Books and the Star Bright Books logo are registered trademarks of Star Bright Books, Inc. Please visit www.starbrightbooks.com.

ISBN-13: 978-1-59572-036-8
ISBN-10: 1-59572-036-7

Printed in China 9 8 7 6 5 4 3 2 1

Library of Congress Cataloging-in-Publication Data is available.

For Arthur and Margie

Dear Santa Claus,

My brother Arthur says there is no Santa Claus and I am wasting my time writing to you but he is wrong lots of times and I know you are really and truly you. I would like you to bring me some ice skates and a new teddy bear cause my old bear Herold has a worn-out belly. And anything else you think a good little girl would like.

Love
Margie

anta Claus
the North Pole

Arthur says that Santa Claus is a big fat humbug. Arthur says he can prove it and I have to help him and it's a secret and if I tell anybody he will put worms in my bed.

Arthur says he is collecting all the stuff we will need to carry out his big plan and we must hide everything until the time is right.

I hung up our stockings and put some cookies and milk on the table cause it is Christmas Eve and I know Santa

Claus will come and he will be hungry when he gets here. Arthur says it's all dumb but Arthur is wrong lots of times.

Arthur says that after Mama and Daddy go to bed it will be time to put his plan into action.

Arthur says I better stay awake or he will put ice cubes in my pajamas.

Arthur says I must tiptoe

quiet as a mouse

and if I make any noise

he will flush Herold

down the toilet.

Arthur says he is making a grand trap to catch a big fat humbug Santa Claus. Arthur put a pail of cold water in the fireplace and a can of pennies by the door.

Arthur tied wind chimes to the Christmas tree and spread balloons all over the floor. Arthur is tying string around everything and hanging bells on it.

Arthur says if I fall asleep he will put bubble gum in my hair.

Arthur says the trap is ready and now we have to wait.

Arthur says maybe he was wrong about Santa Claus

but if I tell anybody he will mush peanut butter and jelly all over Herold's new fur coat.

Dear Santa Claus,

Thank you for the nice ice skates and for the new fuzzy coat for Herold and every thing. I knew you were really and truly you cause Arthur is wrong lots of times.

Love

Margie